This series will feature an
observer robot on lochee park
(But not in this issue)

In another issue there will
be a futuristic go-kart
owned by the A.C.L

More will be made

And someone called Madi going to her
boyfriend's apartment and flipping lots fo
switches on a panel on his coffee table
which changes the room around but then
the sofa she is sitting on flips over!

COPYRIGHT ©
DREW ALOT
ALL RIGHTS RESERVED

This book or parts thereof may not be reproduced in any form, stored in any retrieval system, or transmitted in any form by any means - electronic, mechanical, photocopy, recording or otherwise without prior written permission of the publisher

PAGE 1

CONTENTS

BAD IDEA
by Amanda Wylie
(set in 2014)

We are going to make an army. To hunt this portal pycopath and all the other FREAKS in this world and bring ORDER to this world!
We have collected many of the leftover technology from the alien wars
We're going to be ready to fight back!
We will be known as the Alien control league
THE A.C.L!
.....PAHAHAHAHAH AHAHAHAHAHAH AHA!
THE END?

REVENGE AT LOCHEE SWIMMING BATHS

BY Amanda Wylie set in 2014.

Nice party Laura great turn out

Awww thanks dude

*Lots of people talking

PAGE 5

THE LIGHTS!?
I'll go check them out
*FUZZY NOISE

*FUZZY NOISE

The climbing arena behind me took an incredible fall after an unknown
Power failed to transform the stadium
PAGE 6

It's believed the stadium was adapted from Dronadrone technology
SLAM

YOU!
EVERYONE GET OUT OF HERE!!!!

PAGE 7

AH!

Ugh

*Lot's of people running and panicking

*Electrocuting noise
AAAAH
*Police sirens
THE END?

Time later....
*Police sirens
*Ambulance sirens
PAGE 9

3 Days later....

DRAGONS LAIR

Good afternoon Dragons, my name is Paul Hunter, I'm here looking for 80 million pounds

For a 40% share in my buisness

This should be good
Your uncle just doesn't give up
Allow me to introduce you to the enhanced Alien Control League!
3 DAYS AGO SEVERAL MEDICS DIED VIA ELECTROCUTION TRYING TO SAVE SOMEONE WITH A SUIT MADE FROM ALIEN TECHNOLOGY!
SWOOSH!
Our healthcare workers and police officers are doing a fine job but with limited resources
BUT WHEN THEY FACE A THREAT OUTSIDE THEIR NORMAL SCOPE THEY NEED MORE AND I HAVE PROVIDED IT!!!!
Dragons: PAHAHAHAHAHAHAHA HAHAHAHAHAHAHA!

MAFIA DAD

I can't believe we just got back from 2025! I mean in 2016 I did travel; to 1997 with the QWERTY keyboard but- anyway it's all over now, the whole timeline with your dad being a mafia boss and you and your sisters and brother getting roped into it is all over now, there was actually alot worse stuff in that dark timeline with me getting a cybernetic virus and.....yeah

Voice in head-Blair: Wait Larry bro, probably shouldn't tell Star about becoming a villain in that timeline. Voice in head-Anna: Yeah, and that whole thing with Moonhead and his wife, it's just good it never happened now. Voice in head-Alex: Are you kidding me it was so fun being a villian

Okay, cool, I guess see you Sunday

Yeah YEAH! Cool I guess see you- wait a minute!

DON'T MOVE!

*SIGH

STAB!

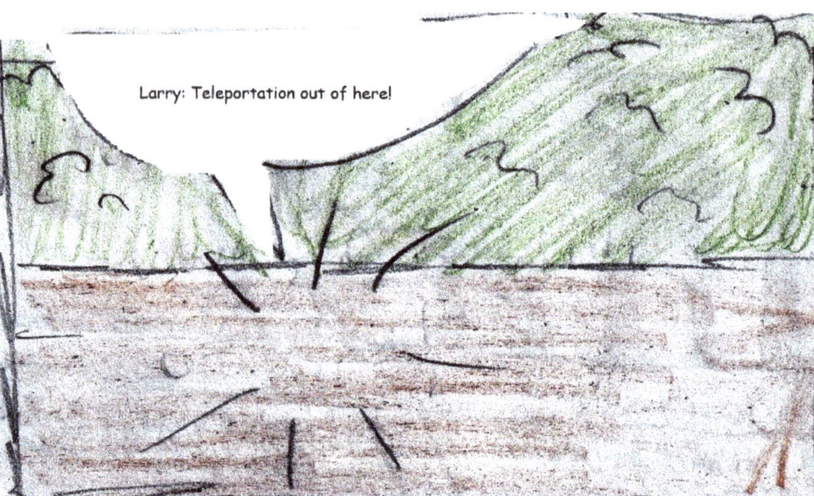
Larry: Teleportation out of here!

Aw you've let him get away. Oh you know, we've had Dranasors, Buttkickers, Portal people, captain cosmic and these Lincolnshire cybernetics switching timelines and, I just need a break, then I'll take out mah nemesis, you're all dismissed, except you Star, you're going to tell me everything about who he is and what was in that timeline he erased

Star's mafia dad spoke to her about how madi seems to have failed. Star was concerned hearing calling and banging from inside a sofa. Star's mafia dad explained it is very important Nevil's dad is taken out and that the fate of all things are at stake

Madi managed to escape! She ran and ran!

Now it was 2020, and mafia dad had sent someone else(Charlie)..... to poison Nevil's dad while his daughter (Summer) snuck into the base!
This is the penthouse, it is legitness

10 Minutes later she died in hospital

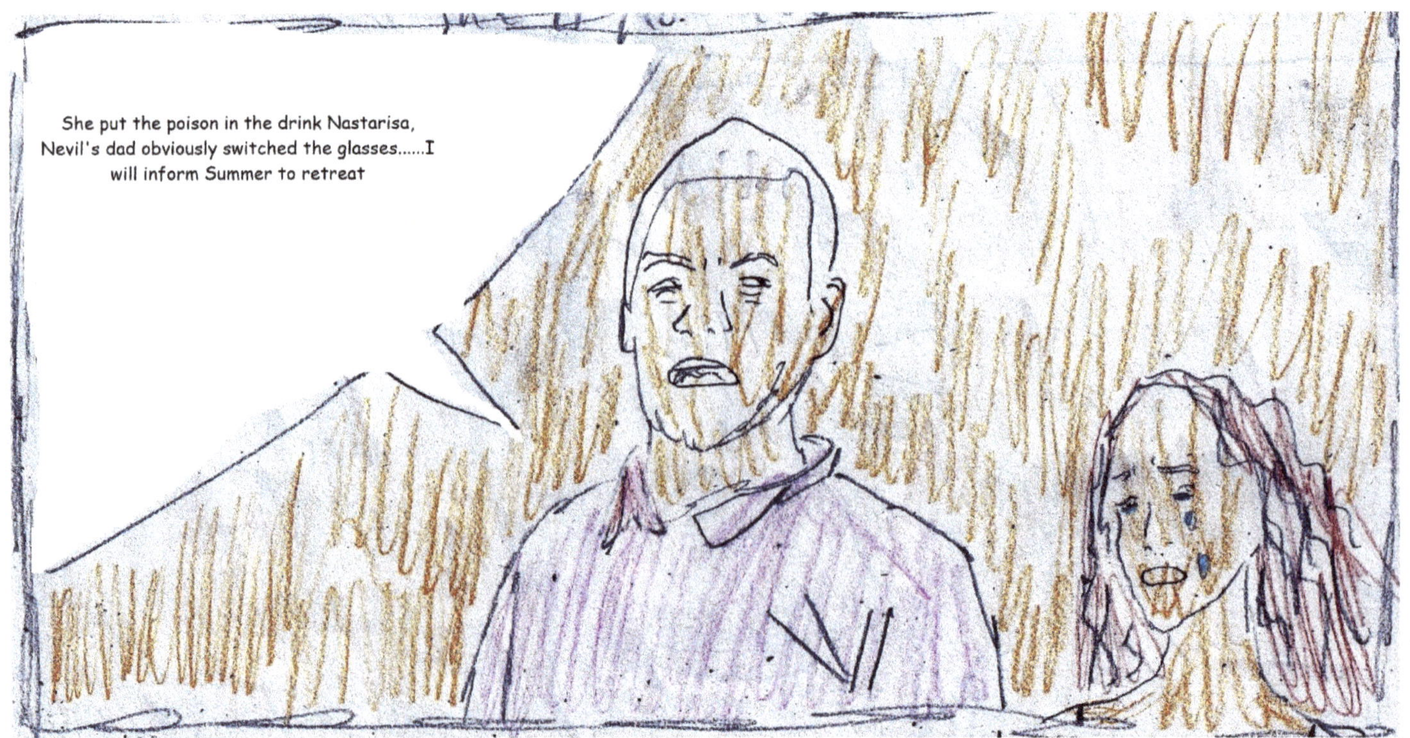
She put the poison in the drink Nastarisa, Nevil's dad obviously switched the glasses......I will inform Summer to retreat

Early 2024

Larry: I stole the universe controller and left a temporary darlkness over Snottinghashire and Lincolnshire!

We are both an enemy of Nevil's dad now

Then I suggest we put our petty rivalries aside and word together

ANOTHER BAD IDEA

I'm in! Let's move forward with this plan!
You'll have your donation by noon today!
ZZZ
Someone hasn't taken his
A.D.H.D meds.........

DESPERATE MEASURES
BY
(set in 2014)
Amanda Wylie
This is getting ridiculous! People in lister flying, a young woman teleporting!?
Sir research shows they all originate from Dundee
Well how is the progress on the A.C.L?
Not good sir! Our equipment is constantly disappearing down a mysterious blue portal, CCTV footage reveals that he is James Perrin, the portal boy!
WHAT!?
*Clenching fists
He must know of our plans.....

We can't do this alone, we need help
I am awake for this!
From who?
Excuse me, I have to make a call
This is the slayer king what do you want?
To see an army rise! I just need you to defend some supplies
There will be a great reward
I'M IN!
THE END?

THESE ADVENTURES WILL CONTINUE